D0513824

This is one of a series of books specially prepared for very young children.

The simple text tells the story of each picture and the bright, colourful illustrations will promote lively discussion between child and adult.

Published by Ladybird Books Ltd Loughborough Leicestershire UK
Ladybird Books Inc Auburn Maine 04210 USA

Printed in England

Ladybird Toddler Books

on
the move

written by LYNNE BRADBURY
illustrated by KEN McKIE

Ladybird Books

See the cars driving along the road.
Some are going fast.
They are overtaking the slower cars.

Here is a tractor
working on a farm.
It is going up and down
the field.

The police car has a flashing light.
It's going very fast.
The siren goes Wah! Wah! Wah! Wah!

The big, fat body of the cement mixer
turns slowly round and round
as it drives along.

Here is a bus full of people.
Some may be going shopping.
The children could be going to school.

The express train is speeding along the rails taking people from town to town. Clicketty clack! Clicketty clack go its wheels!

This huge truck is carrying food
to the shops.
How many wheels can you see?

Look at the ship getting ready
to sail far across the sea.
The little tugboats help it
out of the port.

The motorbike only has
two wheels.
The rider must wear
a crash helmet.

Up in the sky the helicopter flies
over towns and fields.
Its blades go round and round.

The yellow taxi has brought
these people and their suitcases
to an airport.
They must pay for the ride.

This dump truck is full of sand.
Its back tips up and up
and the sand falls out.

e is a bulldozer
elping to make a new road.
t pushes big piles of earth
in front of it.

Look at these cycles.
The bicycle has two wheels.
The tricycle has three wheels.
They are fun to ride.

This is a tanker.
Some tankers go to garages.
Other tankers carry
milk from the farms.

A giant plane like this one
can carry lots of people.
It will fly high in the sky
to places far away.

These ambulances carry
people who are ill.
They will take them to a hospital.

This long train is
moving slowly down the track.
What is the engine pulling?

What is this
scooping up the earth?
It can make very deep holes.

These racing cars
don't drive on ordinary roads.
They race round and round the track.
Which one will win?

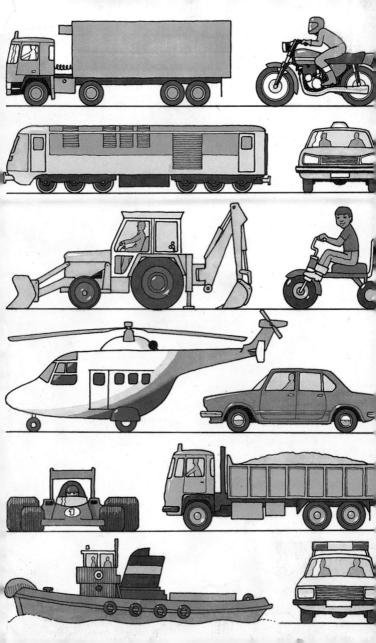